The Bora-Bora Dress

Carole Lexa Schaefer

illustrated by Catherine Stock

CANDLEWICK PRESS
CAMBRIDGE, MASSACHUSETTS

W e're invited to a party," said Mama. "At your fabulous aunt Fiona's on Saturday night."

"Hooray!" said Lindsay. "Aunt Fiona gives the best parties."

"This is a dress-up party," said Mama.

"Yay!" said Lindsay. "I'll wear my pirate suit."

"Not a costume party," said Mama. "A fancy dress-up party."

"I'll wear my ribbon-pocket jeans," said Lindsay.

"Lindsay, this is Aunt Fiona's end-of-the-summer, snazzy, ritzy dress-up party," said Mama. "If you want to go, you'll have to wear a dress."

Lindsay never ever *ever* wore a dress.

She wore her baggy shorts to run on the beach.

She wore her old jeans to climb up to her tree house.

She wore her patch overalls to jump in heaps of leaves.

"What's a dress good for, anyway?" said Lindsay.

"For going to Aunt Fiona's party," said Mama.

Lindsay let Mama take her to Miss Beeline's Girls' Shop
to look — just look — at dresses.

"I'll show you what I have,"
said Miss Beeline. "See here?
A lots-of-dots dress."

"No thanks," said Lindsay.

"A plaid-and-pleats dress."

"Hmm-mm," said Lindsay.

"A fluffy ruffle dress."

"No way!" said Lindsay.

"Lindsay," said Mama, "you pick out a dressing room, and I'll find something for you to try on."

Lindsay wanted to go home. She'd had enough of silly dresses. But she stepped into one of the dressing rooms.

There, on the front of a sundress shaped like a wedge of pie, she spied a parrot in a tree. Lindsay poked it. The cloth crinkled, and the parrot seemed to wink.

"You're nothing but a picture on a dress," said Lindsay.
She poked the parrot again.

Slish—the dress slipped off its hanger. Lindsay read the little tag inside:

Made in Bora-Bora for you.

"Bora-Bora?" said Lindsay. "That sounds far, far away."

The dress felt ripply smooth in her hands. "Made for *me*?" she said, and tried it on.

The dress was as light as butterfly wings.

"*That* dress looks as if it was made for you," said Mama.

"How *could* it be?" said Lindsay. But she agreed to take it home.

Saturday, before Aunt Fiona's party, Lindsay helped color frosting for the tower of teacakes.

"Oooh, Lindsay, your frosting's gorgeous," said Aunt Fiona. "You've used the brightest colors."

"I think," said Lindsay, "that they're the colors of parrot feathers."

After tea, everyone played hide-and-seek in Aunt Fiona's maze garden. "Lindsay, you are the hardest to find," said Mama.

"Am I?" said Lindsay. "That's because I look like a bird in a tree."

On the way down to the beach for moonlight dancing, Lindsay took Aunt Fiona's hand. "Where is Bora-Bora?" she asked.

"In the South Seas. I've been there," said fabulous Aunt Fiona. "It's an island."

"A *magical* island?" said Lindsay. "With winking parrots in flowery trees?"

"Yes," said Aunt Fiona. "And leaping dolphins, and coconut drinks, and people who make wonderful things."

"Maybe," said Lindsay, "somebody there made something wonderful for me."

And the moonlight dancing began.

Lindsay twirled. *Swish swoosh* —the Bora-Bora dress flared out in a circle. The parrot's bright wing flip-flapped. The flowering tree bent and bobbed.

Lindsay fluttered and flitted
and made up a song:

Butterfly girl and parrot
Dance dances they do not know.

Butterfly girl and parrot
Fly as far as they want to go.

Later that night, all ready for bed, Lindsay told Mama, "I sleep best in my striped pajamas."

"You do," said Mama.

"And I run best in my baggy shorts, and climb best in my old jeans, and jump best in my patch overalls."

"Yes," said Mama.

"But at a fancy dress-up party," said Lindsay, "I do everything best in my Bora-Bora dress.

It was made for me, you know."